P9-DGD-741

TABLE OF CONTENTS

THE MYTH, THE LEGEND, THE 'CORN . . .

Greetings, peon! If you're reading this, you must be in way over your head, huh? By now you've likely met those stealthy thieves, the KleptoCats, and their Very Good servants, the KleptoDogs. But if you're reading this (and you haven't accidentally mistaken this for a cookbook), then you must have come in contact with a being far more powerful . . . The rarest of rare creatures, the KleptoCorns (or 'Corns for short).

Follow this book closely, and you may just make it back to your own dimension in one piece.

Before the beginning, before GemDog
and the Very Good Bois, before the
Great Hamster Wars, before even Guapo
himself, there were the KleptoCorns. These
whimsical beings spread scourges of glitter
across the multiverse, stealing sparkly and
sweet things wherever they were to be
found.

With their magical horns, the KleptoCorns could cut portals into the very fabric of reality, which allowed them to quench their thirst for power—and macarons. Sweet, delicious macarons!!! No world was beyond their reach . . . And no being was powerful enough to challenge them.

But, as fate would have it, their powerful gifts were also their greatest curse. For with great power comes great boredom. Wandering the cosmos with only the occasional dying star to amuse them, one of the KleptoCorns, a wise 'Corn named Pipu, happened upon a life-bearing planet that we humans call Earth.

There, it encountered the strangest of species—
felineus meowzeus purrnicum a.k.a. **CATS!**
Approaching with caution, Pipu turned its body
totally invisible, leaving only its magical horn
visible.

Pipu watched as these mysterious creatures engaged in the oddest of rituals: Knocking rand objects off of elevated areas. Clawing at trees a if they were mortal enemies. Even licking their own butts . . . **GROSS!** Though the rest of Pij was invisible, the cats found a primitive sort of fascination with the light from Pipu's horn.

Guapo, First of His Name,* reached out to touc this strange glowing object . . .

great-great-great grandfather of Guapo, current leader of the KleptoCats.

14

When Guapo's paw touched the horn, Pipu was revealed in all its majesty. Pipu saw a grand destiny for Guapo the first, and shared the magic of the portals with the cat. Together, they roamed the galaxy, seeking out both sparkly things and snakes.

A million worlds opened up before Guapo, and the cat soon shared this fearsome power with the rest of its kind. While the cats didn't have invisibility like the KleptoCorns, they were adorable and stealthy.

They quickly put those traits to good use, taking whatever they wanted, and not caring about the consequences.

The KleptoCorns didn't much care about the roving ways of their new feline friends. Since the 'Corns had existed unchallenged for eons, they were now content to observe from afar . . .

GETTING TO KNOW THE KLEPTOCORNS

Much like KleptoCats and KleptoDogs, the KleptoCorns come in many different colors and patterns. KleptoCorns are extremely rare beings, so don't expect to find quite as many of them in any one world. But their incredible powers mean that they're capable of collecting some really good stuff, even if it's a little random. Read on to learn all about the KleptoCorns and their incredible abilities!

★ The Mane Event.

★ Responsible for the teaching of the quantum physics—err, magic—that all KleptoCats and KleptoDogs use to open portals.

★ Lost a left sock? It's got four left feet.

★ Grazes on only the sparkliest of sweets.

★ Has never once painted its hooves; those babies are all natural.

★ Just had its four thousandth birthday and feels great!

GLITTER FALLS

GUMMY

PAKU

- A glutton for shiny things.

- Terrified of clowns, even the colorful, sparkly ones.

- Horses . . . or unicorns . . . shouldn't stretch like that.

- Checkers champion, seven hundred years running.

SUCRE

- The one KleptoCorn that prefers savory dishes.

- Doesn't see the appeal in grazing.

STARDUST

- Enjoys observing the stars—including that pale blue dot.

- Collects disco balls.

- Swears it invented magic.

- Can make anything a competition.

MANA

- Gets nervous when no one's speaking.

- Scared of ferns.

TOKI

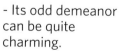

- Its odd demeanor can be quite charming.

- Its abstract art will be analyzed for decades to come.

QUARK

CRYSTAL STAR

SPECTRUM

- All visible colors!
- When in motion, it's impossible to pinpoint the exact color it's wearing at any given moment.

CINDY

- Kleptocorns just want to have fun!
- Everyone knows her from one party or another.

NAMURI

- Hard to tell whether it likes you or not.
- Its close friends keep assuring you it's not mad at you, but can you believe them?

22

RIJU

- Addicted to infomercials.
- Hoarder to the max.

SHADE

- Likes to be with Spectrum because they contrast.
- Mistress of social media.

COODY

- Delivers justice with an impartial hoof.
- The original inspiration for the character of "Javert."

YUNE

- This equine can draw!
- The shapes! The color! The depth! One can't help but marvel at the artistry!

BOTANIUM

GERIN

- Steed of Merlin.
- Such a name dropper.

TRUF

- Quite a rare find.
- Scared of hogs, feral, or otherwise.

GALAXIN

- It's hard to g
a saddle on it
due to its lack
mass.

- I once tried
lean on it and
tripped for a
thousand yea

- A foamy disposition.
- Salt-blooded.

KUMO

CITRUS

- When you approach it, your mouth starts tasting sour.

-Lemons can be deadly around it.

MARTHA

- WHY DID YOU SAY THAT NAME?!

- She could be your mother, you don't know!

MENTITA

- Such a smooth talker.

- With such pleasant breath, it is always ready for smooches.

KLEPTOCORNS 101

At this point, we're sure you're filled with question
Let's begin with a lesson on the KleptoCorns'
abilities.

Portals

KleptoCorns can
open the fabric
of reality using
their horns.
The color of the
portals they open
is notably different
from KleptoCats or
KleptoDogs.

Invisibility

KleptoCorns can
become invisible, and
often use this ability
when stealing things.
The only thing that
remains visible is their
horn.

Minimize / Maximize

KleptoCorns can make objects smaller or larger, a unique ability that allows them to use their horns to take objects of any size. But once a KleptoCorn minimizes an object, they tend to prefer keeping it small. It's just cuter that way, don't you think?

Power up

KleptoCorns recharge their power by eating sparkly and sweet things, or by getting a nice bath and grooming. Be careful, though. Vegetables, caffeine, walnuts, and other food you generally don't find in the candy aisle can make them extraordinarily lethargic.

Beam of Light

KleptoCorns can emit a beam of light from the tip of the horn. This beam can be used to open portals or just to mess around and have fun. In fact, they often use this ability to entertain or lure curious KleptoCats.

WHAT DO KLEPTOCORN WANT?

If that isn't the million-dollar question! By this point, you've probably gathered that KleptoCorns aren't so much mischievous as they are *curious*. These interdimensional beings have been around for quite some time, and things that are new and different are hard to come by. But, in general, KleptoCorns desire . . .

Sparkly, Shiny, Colorful Things:

KleptoCorns love things that are sparkly, shiny, or colorful. They say that all that glitters is not gold, but that doesn't really apply to KleptoCorns. There's nothing more valuable to them than glinting, glimmering, neon objects. Guard your valuables!

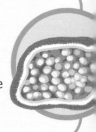

Sweet Things:

KleptoCorns gain their power from sweets, so they're always on the prowl for cake, candy, pudding, macarons, cookies, syrup, and anything else with a high sugar content.

Small Things:

As you've probably inferred from their Minimize/Maximize powers, KleptoCorns love small things, especially when those things were never *meant* to be small. Look for miniaturized buildings, cars, even entire planets that the KleptoCorns have decided look better in miniature.

Cats:

It would seem Pipu was on to something when he taught Guapo the First the ways of the portals. KleptoCorns love to entertain cats with the beam of light from their horns.

. . . Or Really Anything with Big Eyes:

Their love of cute animals doesn't stop with cats. KleptoCorns have been known to collect any adorable creature with big enough eyes. The bigger the better!

Things that Are Yours:

You might be surprised to see a few things you've collected pop up in the clutches of the KleptoCorns. They like things that are weird and different, and you sure have collected a lot of weird and different things, thanks to the help of the KleptoCats and KleptoDogs.

KEEPING KLEPTOCORNS CONTENT

KleptoCorns are curious sorts of creatures—they want to be surrounded by sweet, sparkly things, yes, but they also want to be entertained. And nothing is more entertaining to KleptoCorns than things that are strange and different.

If you're reading this, congratulations! That means *you* are strange and different! This section focuses on keeping these magical beings entertained with your silly human ways. You'll also learn more about what you can expect from life with these fascinating creatures.

KLEPTOCORNS:
EXPECTATIONS vs. REALITY

Expectation: A gorgeous, interdimensional steed to ride across the stars each night.

Reality:
Another night alone with just you and your instant ramen.

KLEPTOCORNS:

Expectation: Treasures beyond your wildest dreams.

Reality: Another bug trapped in gelatin?

LEPTOCORNS:

Expectation: Strange, magical forces at your beck and call.

Reality:
Cleaning up after magical forces.

SPOTTING A KLEPTOCORN POSER

Floppy ears

You can't be serious

Nose is far too small

Dry Skin

Totally the wrong Shape

Too Stout

KLEPTOCORN FOOD GROUPS

Sparkly

Anything that glitters: jewels, glitter sprinkles, sugar.

Shiny

You can see your reflection in it: glazes, frostings, sugar.

Sweet

A particular flavor: commonly found in cakes, desserts, sugar.

Colorful

The brighter the color, the better: macarons, syrups, dyed sugar.

Small

Being able to grab a handful of it and munch away: candies, lollipops, sugar.

Pizza

Because everyone loves pizza, especially with pineapple. Duh.

HOW TO CLEAN UP GLITTER

yeah, that's not going to cut it.

The problem will still be there when you get back.

It's not all gonna fit in that.

On second thought, maybe just give up now.

The hornless, Earth-bound ones.

Vegetables.

The prophecy that they will someday be destroyed by that which they've created.

Caffeine: It puts them to sleep!

THROWING A PARTY FI[T]
FOR A KLEPTOCORN

STEP 1:
Cook up a sparkly feast.

STEP 2:
Add colorful brethren for decoration.

HELPFUL TIP:
Don't offend the 'Corns by eating its candy guts.

STEP 3:

Spice things up with a photo booth.

STEP 4:

Throw out all sense of time. KleptoCorn parties have been known to last for decades.

KLEPTOCORN DOS AND DON'TS

Don't: Present a KleptoCorn with leafy greens. They'll never forgive you. Ever.

Do: Present them with shiny coins (doesn't matter how much they're worth—the shinier, the better). Hello there, Abe!

Don't: Try to summon supernatural beings to help you escape. The KleptoCorns defeated the dragons and the giants; they're not to be challenged.

Do: Amuse KleptoCorns with your desperate escape attempts. The more ridiculous, the better.

BEST USES FOR INVISIBILITY

Sneak attacks.

Setting a trap.

Helping yourself to seconds.

Destroying the evidence.

SPORTS TO NEVER PLAY WITH KLEPTOCORNS

Archery. They might make *you* the target.

Anything equestrian-related (dressage, racing, jumping, polo). KleptoCorns don't understand why the hornless ones allow humans to ride them.

Horseshoes. KleptoCorns take great pride in their hooves. The thought of covering them with strange metal shoes is extremely disturbing.

Really any sport. You don't want to challenge a four thousand year old magical being to anything competitive. They will win, and they will destroy you.

KLEPTOCOURT: ALL RISE FOR THE HONORABLE JUDGE COODY!

Crime: Not sharing the last ice cream bar.

Punishment: Twelve years of community grocery runs.

There are mistakes, but this is pure evil!

Crime: Neglecting your digital pet.

Punishment: Loss of pet custody.

Will allow supervised visitation on the third Friday of every fifth month.

KLEPTOCOURT: ALL RISE FOR THE HONORABLE JUDGE COODY!

Crime: Ignoring a cat in need of being petted.

Punishment: Life . . . in service to KleptoCats.

Shame on you and your wicked ways!

Crime: Giving a KleptoCorn coffee with whipped cream on top.

Punishment: 40 years of hard napping.

How dare you try to trick a KleptoCorn into falling asleep!

FORMING A KLEPTOCORN BAND

Practice makes
perfect. Who needs a
banjo pick when you
have hooves?

Sign with a good agent to make it
onto the radio quickly.

Avoid the paparazzi. (Not always an easy task—even when you can make yourself invisible.)

Music videos are nothing without a proper breeze.

SCIENCE WITH THE KLEPTOCORNS

They say chemistry is like cooking—
just don't lick the spoon.

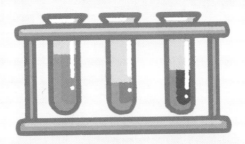

Put a magnet near a kleptoportal
and see how it gets all twisted.

Shrinking the nearest galaxy to fit in a jar has to have some kind of consequences, right? Might not want to get too close . . .

Alchemy has had a few happy accidents, but you best use this to avoid the nasty ones.

KLEPTOCORNS RATE YOUR METHODS OF ESCAPE

Much like your escape attempts, it has training wheels.

0/10

They like where you're going with this, but it's still just a toy.

2/10

This might be rocket-shaped, but you're not getting very far on a children's ride.

5/10

Now we're talking. But without the rest of the suit and a spaceship, we're not sure where you're going with this.

7/10

FOUR KLEPTOCORN OBJECTS THAT AREN'T WHAT YOU THINK

What It Looks Like: A treasure chest.

What It Actually IS: A toilet.

What It Looks Like: A box of bite-sized, tasty snacks.

What It Actually IS: A box of toys.

What It Looks Like: A quantum physics book.

What It Actually IS: A beginner's guide to magic.

What It Looks Like: A bag of magical beans.

What It Actually IS: The path to another war between Giants and KleptoCorns.

KLEPTOCORNS RATE ANIMALS

Tiny Dragon:

The only dragon good enough to avoid being locked up elsewhere in the multiverse.

7/10

Spiky Fren:

Seven percent of all objects shrunk by kleptocorns are made small purely for the purposes of entertaining hedgehogs.

12/10

Kleptocat:

Kleptocats remain the favorite protégés of the Kleptocorns, despite their reign of terror across the galaxy.

Frog:

Barely made the cut for this list. Fortunately, Kleptocorns love anything with big eyes.

GIVE UP YOUR DREAMS TO PLEASE YOUR OVERLORDS

Feed passing KleptoCorns by installing a Dream Catcher.

Inspire the 'Corns' artistic side by letting them paint your dreams in watercolor.

Ringing: A new portal has opened.

Music Box Playing: Used to lure in stray princesses. KleptoCorns love princesses.

MAKING THE MOST OF KLEPTOCORNS

Listen, we'll be the first to empathize with your plight—stranded on a planet light-years from home, with little chance of seeing your loved ones again—but it isn't *all* bad. There are quite a few ways in which being chosen by the 'Corns can benefit you. Read along to discover some of the many ways it helps having the KleptoCorns around.

Nasal mucus from a Kleptocorn is a highly sought-after ingredient.

Perfume professionals have sought the essence of Kleptocorn farts.

NONMAGICAL, PRACTICAL USES FOR HORNS

A chip dispenser: Puncture the bag on their horn and let the chips come to you.

Channeling inner peace.

A place to hang your hat
. . . or ears.

Maintaining
balance.

TREASURE HUNTING WITH KLEPTOCORNS

STEP 1:
Find Map.

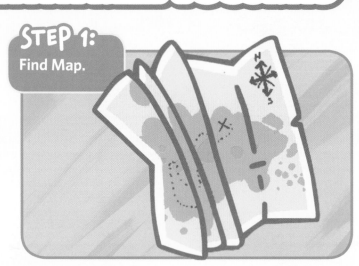

STEP 2:
When in doubt, consult a compass.

STEP 3:

If necessary, get creative . . . or magical. Either one.

STEP 4:

Employ a Good Boi to dig up your loot. Don't be disappointed when it's something weird, like a snow globe.

KLEPTOCORNS' GUIDE TO GOOD VS. BAD FINDS

Bad Find: Curry. Too many flavors for KleptoCorns . . . and none of those flavors are sweet enough to power them.

Good Find: Shiba keychain. It reminds them of the Very Good Shoobs, fighting their good fight in a distant land.

Bad Find: A slice of quiche. It looks like pie, but is most definitely not pie.

Good Find: One Very Good, Lost Boi.

MISSI

GOOD BOI

KLEPTOCORNS' GUIDE TO GOOD VS. BAD FINDS

Good Find: Summoner's staff. KleptoCorns would hate for that to get into the wrong hands, though it would certainly make things interesting for a change . . .

Bad Find: A swing, when there's no one there to push you.

Good Find: Ice cream. There is never a bad time for ice cream.

Bad Find: A sign for ice cream. How are the 'Corns supposed to find ice cream now that someone's stolen the sign?!

KLEPTOCORNS' GUIDE TO HORTICULTURE

Start out with something simple. Some plants only need a little water and love.

Don't be afraid if your plants don't always grow straight. Let them find their own way.

Also don't be afraid if your plants eat people. As long as they don't eat you, it's okay.

Reap the fruits of your labor, even if they are a little strange.

THE MANE EVENT

Some KleptoCorns just naturally complement each other's style.

Don't be intimidated by complex, braided hairdos. There's only a twenty-six percent chance of spontaneous combustion when braiding a KleptoCorn's mane, so the odds of survival are in your favor!

Don't fight a KleptoCorn's natural mane, though: You could end up in another dimension.

When in doubt, a fun new color (or several) can really liven up a look.

EXERCISING YOUR KLEPTOCORNS

Set some good music.

Start with something simple, like jumping jacks.

Advanced dance moves are to be avoided at all costs. Trust us—you're not ready for this jelly.

Don't forget the cooldown.

WHY THE KLEPTOCORNS COULD EASILY DESTROY ANY CIVILIZATION

Ever see their laser horns at full power? You might need these.

Adorableness + Absolute Cosmic Power = No Chance for Resistance

Anyone who disagrees with their new world order can be dropped into another dimension.

Did you forget about their shrinking powers? Nothing is really intimidating at one-tenth its normal size.

COMMON KLEPTOCORNS COMPLAINTS AND HOW TO SOLVE THEM

Complaint: Blurry vision.

Solution: Corrective kaleidoscope glasses.

Complaint: Too fabulous for this world.

Solution: Try another world.

Complaint: Suboptimal frozen treat design.

Solution: Optimal frozen treat design.

Complaint: No good music to listen to.

Solution: Create your own.

COOKING WITH KLEPTOCORNS

We're not saying you could actually eat any of this, but your 'Corns could!

Magnesium

Nutritious, though not delicious. The kale of gemstones. Better when marinated in stardust.

Bismuth

Is it the tastiest gem? That's up for debate, but it's all the more prized for its rarity.

Amber

The mystery meat of gemstones—you never know what organic matter might be trapped inside.

Sapphire

KleptoCorns cry sapphire tears, so this gem isn't commonly eaten by them . . . Except maybe the melodramatic ones.

Opal

Opals come in countless flavors, so be sure to pick the right ones.

Tetrahedrite

Increases your chances of adventure by thirty-one percent. Not to be eaten by the faint of heart.

Topaz

Add this handsome spice to any dish for instant pizzazz.

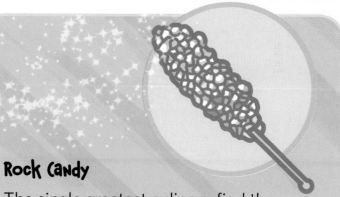

Rock Candy

The single greatest culinary find the KleptoCorns ever made. More delicious crystals do not exist in this or any other dimension.

NEW CANDIDATES FOR PORTAL MAGIC

KleptoFoxes

Verdict: Too tricky. Not to be trusted with portal magic.

KleptoOwls

Verdict: Their inquisitive nature makes them a possibility.

KleptoElephants

Verdict: With a memory like that, they're bound to use their powers to even far too many scores.

KleptoAliens

Verdict: They seem to be doing fine on their own. Why rock the boat?

KLEPTOCORNS RATE DEEP SEA CREATURES

Jellyfish:

Always jealous. Who needs that kind of negativity?

4/10

Trilobite:

Brought back from a prehistoric time to satisfy Kleptocorns' curiosity. They weren't disappointed.

11/10

Cuttlefish:

A little too carefree for their tastes.

7/10

Oyster:

Silent and it turns dirt into delectable, shiny stones? Count us in.

15/10

PRACTICAL USES FOR GOLD (AS WRITTEN BY KLEPTOCORNS)

Defense from aerial attackers.

A bridle of sorts for humans.

A maker of princesses.

Camouflage from magical beings.

CONGRATULATIONS, PEON!

You've made it to the end of this guide, which means you're ready to take your first steps into intergalactic domination . . . behind your all-powerful friends. As you embark on this new journey, remember your five B's:

⭐ Don't **Brush** KleptoCorns. Their mane could cause you to spontaneously combust.

⭐ Don't feed KleptoCorns **Beans**. They hate non-sweet/sparkly things, and trust us, you don't want to know about their farts.

⭐ Don't try to **Break Out** of your new home. At best it will amuse your overlords; at worst, it'll get you into a whole mess of trouble.

⭐ Don't bring **Bears** into the equation. They won't fight for you and they should really be left alone, you know?

⭐ Don't **Binge** KleptoCorns' food. Not all of it is edible to humans, and the stuff that is really isn't very healthy for you. Plus you should really learn to share.

UNTIL NEXT TIME, UNDERLINGS!

ISBN 978-1-338-60632-4

10 9 8 7 6 5 4 3 2 1

20 21 22 23 24

40

Printed in the U.S.A.
First printing 2020

Book design by Jessica Meltzer and Becky James

KLEPT CORNS

SURVIVING THE SPARKLE!

OFFICIAL GUIDE TO
ALL THAT GLITTERS

By Daphne Pendergrass

Scholastic Inc.